Marie Décary

Adam's Tropical Adventure

Illustrated by Steve Beshwaty
Translated by Sarah Cummins

First Novels

W9-BYK-842

Formac Publishing Company Limited
Halifax, Nova Scotia

Originally published as *Un oiseau rare*

Copyright © 2004 Les éditions de la courte échelle inc.

Translation Copyright © 2005 Sarah Cummins

Formac Publishing Company Limited acknowledges the support of the Culture Division, Nova Scotia Department of Tourism, Culture and Heritage. We acknowledge the financial support of the Government of Canada through the Book Publishing Industry Development Program (BPIDP) for our publishing activities.

We acknowledge the support of the Canada Council for the Arts for our publishing program.

Library and Archives Canada Cataloguing in Publication

Décary, Marie

[Oiseau rare. English]
    Adam's tropical adventure / by Marie Décary ; illustrated by Steve Beshwaty ; translated by Sarah Cummins.
(First novels ; 56)
Translation of: Un oiseau rare.

ISBN 0-88780-687-2 (bound)   ISBN 0-88780-686-4 (pbk.)
    I. Cummins, Sarah II. Beshwaty, Steve III. Title. IV. Series.
PS8557.E235O4713 2005   jC843'.54   C2005-904621-X

Formac Publishing
Company Limited
5502 Atlantic Street
Halifax, Nova Scotia B3H 1G4
www.formac.ca

Distributed in the United States by:
Orca Book Publishers
P.O. Box 468
Custer, WA
USA 98240-0468

Printed and bound in Canada

Adam's Tropical Adventure

Table of Contents

1
Higher than the Clouds

Monday is not usually a very exciting day. The weekend is over and the next Saturday still seems very far off.

But that Monday evening Adam was as happy as a flea on a dog! He was wiggling and wriggling and hopping with excitement.

Why? Because it was his grandmother Zoë's birthday. Adam loved Zoë, mainly because she treated him like a grown-up. And also because whenever she came to visit, Zoë always had a surprise for him.

Adam was flying high, but now it

was time for him to return to Earth, back to the dining room — where his parents — Alex and Annie — and his grandmother were sitting around the table.

On the table there was a birthday cake, of course. It was a towering layer cake, made of zucchini and flax seeds.

What a cake! But Zoë would never complain, for she loved all growing things. No wonder she had been a reporter for the magazine *The Green Life* for thirty years.

"Hap-py Birth-day, dear Zo-ë!" sang Adam and his parents.

Zoë was happy and pleased. You could see it on her face. Her cheeks were as pink as a strawberry jellybean. She took a deep breath and blew out

her candles, quite a feat considering there were fifty-five of them.

"Guess what!" said Zoë, digging into her cake. "*The Green Life* is sending me on vacation to Discovery Island."

"Where's that?" Adam asked.

Zoë gave Annie and Alex a secret smile. Then she placed her hand over Adam's.

"It's a tiny, wild island in the middle of nowhere on the other side of the world," she said. "To get there, you

have to take two airplanes."

"*Two* airplanes!" Adam was intrigued.

With shining eyes, Zoë told him about the trip she had planned. In his mind, he could see the blue-green ocean with its fluorescent fish, the waterfall, the jungle…

Whoa! Adam was already soaring high above the clouds. Zoë's next words took him even higher. "It would be the best present ever if you could come with me, Adam."

Adam's eyes grew bigger than a cartoon character's eyes.

"Yes! Yes! I'll come with you!"

He jumped up for joy and gave Zoë a kiss on each of her rosy cheeks. Adam was ready to pack his bags that instant. But what would his parents have to say?

"Surprise!" said his dad.

And he handed Adam a brand-new backpack. Inside were outdoor adventure clothes, a notebook and pencil, and a camera.

"You never know," said his mother. "You might want to learn to be a reporter too."

"Like your favourite character, Tintin," said his dad. "But instead of Snowy, you'll have Zoë."

"Wow!" cried Adam, delighted.

2
Click! Click! Click!

Four Mondays later, Adam and Zoë
finally landed on Discovery Island.

Of course, Adam had his camera
hanging from a strap around his neck.
His notebook was in his pocket and his
pencil was behind his ear. He obviously
took his job as reporter very seriously.

As soon as they arrived at Crusoe's
Bed & Breakfast, they hurried to meet
the owner. With his white beard and
deeply tanned skin, Mr. Robinson
looked as if he had lived on Discovery
Island for a long time.

"Is there anything interesting here?" asked Adam.

Mr. Robinson burst out laughing.

"Discovery Island is one of the last corners of paradise left on earth, my boy," he declared proudly.

Adam was not impressed. This information didn't seem very exciting. While his grandmother continued to chat with Mr. Robinson, he headed towards a trail lined with coconut palms.

Adam saw a few lizards running off as he approached. Click! A couple of panicky crabs. Click! Some ants marching ten by ten. Click!

Since he was keeping his eyes on the path, Adam didn't really know where he was going. Suddenly the sea was there before him, a sheet of

sparkling turquoise. Now that was
worth a photo!

Darn! As Adam looked through his
viewfinder, what did he see? Two
intruders blocking his view! A boy and
girl, both with hair hanging down in
many little braids, both wearing
oversize T-shirts. They looked like
twins.

"We're called the Doubles," said the girl. "My name is Aïda and this is my brother Gaspard. Are you going to write about us in your newspaper?"

Adam was flattered that they thought he was a real reporter. He decided to go along with the idea.

"That depends! If you help me get a scoop, for sure I will!"

Gaspard and Aïda looked puzzled. Now Adam was sure he could fool them. He explained that a scoop was a hot news item — so hot that it would amaze everyone in the whole world.

"We'll go into the jungle then," suggested Gaspard. "Unless you're afraid of the Varmint…"

Now it was Adam's turn to be puzzled.

"Don't worry," said Aïda reassuringly. "Sometimes the Varmint prowls around the mountainside. But he spends most of his time sleeping or picking his nose."

"But anyway, bye! See you tomorrow morning!" cried Gaspard.

With that, the Doubles disappeared. Night had fallen on the deserted beach and it was as dark as the inside of a jar of molasses. Fortunately, Zoë was not far off.

"I've been looking for you everywhere," she panted as she ran up to Adam.

"I met two kids," explained Adam. "They have some things to show me...for my reporting."

"Are they Mr. Robinson's

grandchildren? They will probably be good guides, since they know the island very well."

On the path leading back to their ocean-front hut, Zoë added, "A reporter's first job is to get information!"

3
A Rare Bird

The next morning Adam had no trouble waking up, and even less trouble getting ready for the day, since he had slept in his clothes.

He heard a whisper through the window. "Psst! We're waiting for you outside." It was the Doubles.

Adam picked up his notebook and his pencil. Where was his camera? He couldn't find it among the things from his half-unpacked suitcases. Too bad!

Before he left, Adam scribbled on a piece of paper: *Gone looking for a scoop with Aïda and Gaspard.*

He slipped this message under Zoë's pillow. She was still sleeping like a baby. Adam tiptoed out.

As the sun's first rays kissed the ocean, Adam, Gaspard, and Aïda headed for the mountain.

"This way!" ordered Aïda, pointing to a muddy trail.

The Doubles, who were barefoot, ran on ahead. Adam tried to catch up, but it was hopeless! In his plastic sandals, all he could do was skid from tree root to thorny bush.

"Wait up!" he called.

After less than a minute in the jungle, Adam felt as tiny as a leprechaun in a land of giant trees. To stave off panic, he took out his notebook and pencil.

Now, there was something strange. He noticed a patch of red way up in the highest branches. It looked like a banner floating in the breeze.

Suddenly the banner took off. It glided for a distance then began to dive — straight towards Adam! He had only enough time to note that the flying object had a head, wings, and claws.

"Aaagh!" he yelled, covering his face.

Whew! He was safe. But his head had become a roost. Long red feathers dangled in front of his nose.

"Roocoocooroocoo," the bird sang sweetly.

The only birds Adam knew were sparrows, so he answered the best he could: "Peet-peet-peet."

The feathered beast seemed
enchanted with his reply. It jumped
onto Adam's shoulder and began to
peck at his neck and ears and chin.

"Hey! Stop it!" begged Adam, laughing. "That tickles!"

Suddenly, the incredible bird snatched Adam's pencil in its beak and flew off!

Adam watched in amazement as it disappeared in the distance. Finally all he could see was a little red dot in the blue sky.

"Were you frightened?" asked Gaspard, appearing from a thicket and smiling.

"No. A good reporter keeps his wits about him. But I have something to tell you."

Adam pointed out the tree and described the fabulous bird. He even imitated its song.

"He saw a roocoocoo!" exclaimed Aïda.

"No way!" said Gaspard. "There are none left on the island."

Adam was about to answer when a terrifying *crack!* made all three of them jump.

"Run!" yelled Aïda. "It's the Varmint!"

4
A Visit to the Museum

When he got back to Crusoe's, Adam was splattered with mud up to his eyebrows. Zoë was waiting for him on the veranda. As soon as he saw her, Adam realized that his grandmother had been worried.

"I saw a rare bird," he explained.

"He really did!" Aïda said, appearing with her brother and her grandfather.

"If you actually saw a *Rukukus exoticus ruber*, that is indeed very important news," Mr. Robinson confirmed.

Then he said he wanted to show them all something.

"Welcome to the museum," he said, pushing open the door to a sort of wooden shack.

He disappeared into a dark corner. Adam could hear him moving a table, opening cupboards, rattling pots and pans.

When he finally reappeared, draped in cobwebs, he was carrying a stuffed animal. Although the red plumage was faded and the eyes were glass, Adam recognized the roocoocoo.

"That's it," he said. "But I saw a live one."

Mr. Robinson gave a sigh of delight. He asked Zoë and Adam to take a seat on a bench. He had Aïda and Gaspard stand on either side of him. Then he began to tell a story. It almost seemed like a legend.

"A long, long time ago, a solitary sailor landed on our island. This man, a poet, had been driven from his own country because his ideas displeased the king."

Mr. Robinson raised his index finger like a professor giving a lecture.

"Before exiling his undesirable subject, the king granted him two favours."

"I know!" cried Aïda. "The poet was allowed to bring crates of paper and pencils with him. And also his two white birds."

Gaspard continued the story, saying that the roocoocoos had adapted well to

their new environment. And since they now ate shrimp and berries, their feathers had turned red.

"That's impossible," protested Adam.

"The same thing happens to pink flamingos," explained Zoë. "Why not roocoocoos too?"

"Exactly!" said Mr. Robinson. "After the poet's death, the roocoocoos multiplied. There used to be thousands of them on our island."

"So why are they all gone?" asked Adam.

"Over time, the inhabitants of Discovery Island began to hunt them. For food, or to sell their feathers."

"And now the roocoocoo is considered to be extinct," added Aïda.

Suddenly Mr. Robinson didn't seem happy that a roocoocoo had been found. He looked worried.

"The problem is that the Varmint is going to be interested in this," he told them. "Last year he pulled up a plant that was on the endangered species list, a *Cactus spinosus*. He was going to sell it to foreigners."

5
Tracking the Roocoocoo

Ever since he found out his rare bird was threatened, Adam was worried. And he wasn't the only one.

"The roocoocoo is affectionate and easy to tame," said Aïda.

"And way too easy to catch," added Gaspard.

Zoë was trying to calm their fears when Mr. Robinson came down from the mountain.

"I found the nest," he panted. "It was empty. Quick, we have to go over to the Varmint's place. He's probably already captured the poor thing."

Adam ran to get his camera, and this time he put on his all-terrain shoes. Gaspard brought the stuffed bird and Aïda fetched an old tape recorder from the museum.

"If we have to, we'll make a fake roocoocoo to trick the bandit," explained Gaspard. He put everything in a canvas bag.

"Is everybody ready?" asked Mr. Robinson.

Yes! The five of them crammed into his electric car and headed off to Pirates Bay, where the Varmint was plotting his evil deeds.

When they got there, Adam was surprised to find that the Varmint lived in an old tin shack in the middle of a dump. As he was looking around,

Adam spied a little piece of wood lying on the ground.

"My pencil!" he cried. "The roocoocoo can't be far away."

The others were too busy looking around and peering at the shack to ask any questions.

"The only window in the shack is two metres off the ground," observed Zoë. "And we have no ladder."

"I have an idea," Gaspard piped up.

He suggested that Adam climb up on his shoulders. Staggering, he carried Adam over to the window.

Adam was right under the opening. He couldn't see inside, so he listened.

The first thing he heard was loud snoring. Then a phone rang. Adam heard someone grunt and answer it.

"Yeah, I caught 'em. The male and the female. Two roocoocoos are better than one!"

Adam was so mad he thought he would explode! But he wanted to hear the rest.

"I can deliver them anytime," said the bandit to his accomplice. "Okay, see you in the Bay at sunset."

Adam signalled to Gaspard to let him down. They ran back to the others and Adam repeated word-for-word all that he had heard.

"I have a plan," said Zoë. "How much time do we have until sunset?"

Mr. Robinson lifted his eyes to the sky as if he was looking at his watch.

"Thirty minutes and three seconds," he announced.

6
Operation Rescue!

While Zoë outlined her plan, Mr.
Robinson was busy drawing a map in
the sand. The Varmint's shack was a
square. Pirates Bay was a half-circle.
Between the two of them he drew
paths, which the children studied
carefully.

"There! Good luck, everybody!"
said Zoë.

Step 1: Zoë slung Adam's camera
around her neck and strode over to the
shack. *Plang! Plang!* She knocked on
the door.

The Varmint opened it. He was a

sight to see, with one finger stuck up his nose.

"Hello, my name is Zoë Knight. I'm a journalist." Zöe calmly introduced herself and started to spin out her patter. Blahblahblah.

Great! The Varmint fell into the trap and started answering her questions. Adam watched from a distance as his grandmother led the villain from his lair.

Step 2: Mr. Robinson hurried down to the village to warn Arnold, the island's only policeman.

Meanwhile, Adam and the Doubles ran to the shack and went inside. Once their eyes got used to the dark, they began their search.

"Over here!" whispered Gaspard.

Under a tattered mattress and a pile of filthy clothing, they found a suspicious banana crate. Adam untied the rope that held the cover on and

lifted it up. Aha! The two roocoocoos were inside. Their beaks were held shut with elastic bands, so they couldn't sing. But they were alive!

"They're so beautiful," cooed Aïda as she cradled them in her long T-shirt.

Step 3: Gaspard pulled the stuffed bird from the bag and placed it in the crate. He put the tape recorder next to it. "Roocoocooroocoo," it went, then it stopped.

"It does that every 15 minutes," Gaspard said.

Step 4: The three children took a secret path back to the dune where Zoë was hiding, having finished her fake interview.

"When I left our enemy, he was returning to his shack," she told them.

"He should be here soon."

He was! The Varmint appeared on the beach, carrying the crate under his arm.

After looking all around, he walked out along the old dock. He stepped onto his accomplice's yacht and handed over the goods. Then he held out his hand for his loot.

Of course, when the smuggler opened the crate to check, his mouth fell open in surprise. As Gaspard had planned, the tape started playing just then.

"Roocoocooroocoo!"

"What is this, some kind of a joke?" the smuggler spat out.

Then the Varmint and his partner started fighting. From their observation post, Zoë, Adam, and the Doubles watched the two bandits yell and push and hit each other.

"You slimy scumbags!" someone roared. It was Arnold, the policeman.

Unbelievable! His voice was so powerful that it knocked the two crooks into the water. *Sploosh!* All Arnold had to do was pull them out like a couple of big fish and put the handcuffs on. Quite a catch!

From behind the dune, Zoë immortalized their capture on film. Click! The jolly band laughed and laughed.

"Hooray! I got my scoop!" cried Adam.

7
Once a Reporter,
Always a Reporter

What a party there was that night at Crusoe's! Zoë brought fruit punch for everyone. Adam and the Doubles had fun remembering every second of their day. The roocoocoos jumped from one head to another, to say thank-you for the rescue.

"Bravo! Mission accomplished!" declared Mr. Robinson.

"And tomorrow, we'll go swimming in the falls," Gaspard promised Adam.

"I want to braid your hair," Aïda told him. "Then we can be the Triples!"

"Not right now," Adam excused himself. "I have to write my story. But you can be sure I'll write about you!"

He went down to the beach and took his pencil from his pocket. The pair of roocoocoos came and sat on the sand near him. As he gazed at their fiery red plumage and their mischievous eyes, inspiration came to him.

*　　*　　*

Three months later, Zoë arrived at Adam's house with the latest issue of *The Green Life*.

Adam's dad was even more excited than Adam was. He snatched up the magazine. Adam's mom stood on her tiptoes and tried to look at the pictures over his shoulder.

Alex proudly read aloud the introduction that the editor-in-chief had written.

Thanks to timely action by our young reporter, Adam Knight, two poachers involved in trafficking exotic birds have been exposed. And the Rukukus exoticus ruber *is now on the planet's list of protected species.*

"Let me read the story I wrote," Adam said, taking the magazine.

Some people have forgotten that the earth belongs to the children of today and the future. My voyage to Discovery Island allowed me to take action for change. But I could never have succeeded without my friends Aïda and Gaspard.

When I am as old as Mr. Robinson, I hope there will be thousands of roocoocoos on Discovery Island, as there were before and hopefully will be forever.

Adam lifted his eyes from the page and looked at Zoë. Then he went on:

I thank my grandmother Zoë for taking me on the best vacation of my life. Our wonderful adventure has

given us something that we will share
our whole life long —

Adam squinted at the next word. He repeated the phrase, making sure to articulate each word.

…something we will share our whole life long: inedible memories!

"I think you mean *indelible*," his mother corrected him.

"Whatever!" laughed Zoë. "The day I decide to retire, I know who can take over my job."

"Roocoocooroocoo!" sang Adam happily.

Three more new novels in the *First Novels Series*!

Maddie Stands Tall

Louise Leblanc
Illustrated by Marie-Louise Gay
Translated by Sarah Cummins

When Maddie finds out that her little brother, Julian, is being terrorized by a group of bullies at school, she decides that her gang should confront the problem head-on. Julian, however, has been staying home from school, sick with fear. When he finds out that Maddie is going to fight the bullies, he tells all.

In this story, Maddie comes up with a solution to stop the fighting, fear and silence.

Toby Shoots for Infinity

Jean Lemieux
Illustrated by Sophie Casson
Translated by Sarah Cummins

Toby wants to know what there is at the end of the universe. When he finds out that there is only infinity, he wants to find the answer to a question that his parents cannot answer. To do this, Toby tries to get to infinity by counting, with a little help from his friends, parents and teachers along the way.

In this story, Toby discovers that everyone has a different approach to questions that have no definite answer.

Fred and the Mysterious Letter

Marie-Danielle Croteau
Illustrated by Bruno St-Aubin
Translated by Sarah Cummins

When Fred gets a letter from his secret crush, Lola, he is too excited to open it immediately. Unfortunately, his cat, Rick, shreds the letter before he can read it and he can't make sense of it when he tries to put it back together. Fred's grandmother offers to help him unravel the mystery.

In this story, Fred learns about the value of hope and perseverance.

Meet all the great kids in the *First Novels Series!*

Formac Publishing Company Limited

5502 Atlantic Street, Halifax, Nova Scotia   B3H 1G4

Orders: 1-800-565-1975 Fax: 902-425-0166

www.formac.ca